*For Ripley — who sleeps with his eyes open — and for Chris,
with love — T.H.*

To Timolin, Melissa and Jeff — A. & L.D.

Text copyright © 1999 by Troon Harrison
Illustrations copyright © 1999 by Alan and Lea Daniel

We acknowledge the support of the Canada Council for the Arts and the
Ontario Arts Council for our publishing program.

Published in Canada by	Published in the U.S. by
Kids Can Press Ltd.	Kids Can Press Ltd.
29 Birch Avenue	85 River Rock Drive, Suite 202
Toronto, ON M4V 1E2	Buffalo, NY 14207

The artwork in this book was rendered in
mixed media, primarily acrylic.
Text is set in Palatino.

Edited by Debbie Rogosin
Designed by Marie Bartholomew
Printed in Hong Kong by Book Art Inc., Toronto

CM 99 0 9 8 7 6 5 4 3 2 1

Canadian Cataloguing in Publication Data

Harrison, Troon
        The dream collector

ISBN 1-55074-437-2

I. Daniel, Alan, 1939-   II. Daniel, Lea.   III. Title.

PS8565.A6587D73   1999   jC813'.54   C97-932650-8
PZ7.H37Dr   1999

The
Dream Collector

Written by
Troon Harrison

Illustrated by
Alan and Lea Daniel

Kids Can Press

Quite early, before anyone else was awake, Zachary saw that it was going to be an extraordinary Saturday. Two zebras and a huge shaggy dog were drinking from the birdbath. Zachary had been asking his parents for months if he could have a dog like that.

"Wait for me!" he shouted, pulling on his sneakers.

The zebras galloped away through the flowers when Zachary opened the door. The dog chased after them. As Zachary started to follow he noticed another unusual thing. At the end of his driveway was a truck with dusty fenders. A short man was standing on a crate, looking under the hood. He wore overalls with shiny buttons.

"Good morning," said Zachary. "Who are you?"

"Read the door panel," suggested the man with a chuckle.

"Dream Collector. Streets Clear by Dawn." Zachary read the lettering aloud. "What does that mean?" he wondered.

The Dream Collector pulled his head out from under the hood and smiled. He had cheeks the color of old plums and eyes as blue as summer afternoons. "Have you ever thought about what happens to your dreams?" he asked Zachary.

Zachary shook his head.

"You haven't? Well, I come around at dawn and collect them. It's city regulations," the Dream Collector explained.

"Wow! What happens if you don't collect the dreams?" asked Zachary.

"That would be a disaster!" exclaimed the Dream Collector. "The closer it gets to morning, the more real the dreams become. Once sunlight touches them, they're here to stay. Imagine! The whole neighborhood would be overrun with dreams!"

At that moment two pirates strolled down the driveway.

"Were they someone's dream?" asked Zachary.

"Yes," replied the Dream Collector as he poked his head back under the hood.

Zachary heard him mutter something about piston rings. "Is your truck broken down?" he asked.

"It is. It won't start and I've forgotten my toolbox." The Dream Collector sounded worried.

"I can get some tools," offered Zachary. "What do you need?"

"Can you find a spark-plug wrench, a battery tester and a socket set?"

Zachary ran into the garage and looked at his dad's tools. He wasn't too sure what some of them were called. The only sock set he could find was a pair he had taken off after a ball game. He hoped the Dream Collector wouldn't think they were too dirty to use. Zachary found the battery tester, but he didn't know which wrench was the right one. He took a variety so the Dream Collector could choose the one he needed.

Just as Zachary reached the truck, the shaggy dog dashed by chasing three rabbits. "Hey, that dog was *my* dream!" exclaimed Zachary in astonishment. "I wish I had a dog like that."

By now there were dreams everywhere. The Dream Collector looked around anxiously. "The street should be clear already," he moaned. "Soon the sun will be up. This is serious."

He chose a wrench from Zachary's collection. Zachary thought it was too small to use on such a big truck. He hoped the Dream Collector knew what he was doing.

"Can I help you fix the truck?" Zachary asked. "Once, I fixed my mom's vacuum cleaner after it sucked up some toys."

The Dream Collector chuckled. "Trucks and vacuums are very different inside. But maybe you can do another special job for me."

"What?" asked Zachary.

"Perhaps you can load the dreams into the truck. Some dreams, like dogs, might be hard to catch though," he said, with a twinkle in his eye. "Do you think you can do it?"

"Oh yes, I can do that," Zachary said proudly.

Zachary crept into the house and carefully chose the things he'd need to catch the dreams. When he came back out the sun was rising. He would have to move fast.

The carrots and the lasso worked fine, and soon the zebras were in the truck. The parrots liked the shiny whistle.

"This job is easy," said Zachary. " Now I'll look for the shaggy dog."

Zachary heard barking in a neighbor's yard and went to investigate. The dog was jumping at smoke rings blown by a scaly dragon.

Just then a knight wandered into the yard. Seeing the dragon, he drew his sword. The dog dashed away.

"Come back," called Zachary, but the dog kept running.

When the knight brandished his sword, the dragon turned pale with fright. Luckily, at that moment a huge horse trotted out from the roses. The knight sheathed his blade and happily put his arms around the horse's neck.

"Whew," whispered Zachary, "that was close."

Now the yard was crowded with dreams.

"Follow me everyone!" Zachary called, leading the way.

One by one, the dreams climbed the ramp into the truck. Zachary gave a sigh of relief. Only the dog was still missing.

Zachary walked down the street again, whistling for it. The dog barked from somewhere in the bushes.

"Come on out!" called Zachary, pushing aside branches. But the dog had disappeared.

Sunlight was touching the treetops. Zachary decided he'd better talk to the Dream Collector.

"Is the truck nearly fixed?" he asked. "We're running out of time."

"We are, but I can't find the problem," replied the Dream Collector. He chose a different wrench.

Zachary sat on the bumper. "You know what?" he asked. "I always sleep with my eyes open so I can see my dreams going by in the dark. Once, I dreamed about a rhinoceros."

"I remember," answered the Dream Collector. "It was such a heavy beast I thought my truck springs would break. We'll have to make a deal sometime, Zachary, about no more rhinoceros dreams."

"Maybe." Zachary smiled.

While the Dream Collector tried out wrenches, Zachary searched for the dog. He looked around toolsheds and greenhouses, under trucks and behind trees. Then he saw dirt flying. He leaped toward the dog but it leaped faster. Zachary scrambled out of the dog's hole with dirt between his teeth.

There was no sign of the dog.

Maybe it likes this street, thought Zachary. Maybe it doesn't want to leave.

Sunlight was shining on the front windows of all the houses. Zachary went to tell the Dream Collector that one dream was still on the loose.

"Stand back!" warned the Dream Collector when Zachary appeared. "I'm going to try starting the truck."

Zachary stepped out of the way. There was a long pause. The knight's horse neighed. Then the engine burst into life with a magnificent roar. It was just in time. Sunlight was flooding the street.

"Hurrah!" shouted the Dream Collector. "Thanks for your help. I couldn't have managed without you!"

"I can't find the dog!" called Zachary.

The Dream Collector gave a piercing whistle and the shaggy dog bounded from the bushes. It looked exactly the way Zachary thought a dog should look, with a drooping mustache and eyes like chocolate kisses. When the dog wagged its tail its hind feet almost lifted off the ground.

"Think you'd like this dog?" asked the Dream Collector.

"I'd love this dog," replied Zachary.

"Then it's yours," said the Dream Collector. "It will be even more fun than fixing vacuum cleaners."

Zachary let out a whoop. He could hardly believe his luck. "Thank you!" he shouted.

The Dream Collector released the brakes and waved. "How about a deal?" he called. "No more rhinoceroses!"

"It's a deal!" Zachary laughed as the truck rumbled away on its sagging springs.

Zachary took his wonderful, dream-come-true dog by the collar, and together they ran up the driveway.

"Let's go and jump on Mom and Dad's bed," Zachary said. "They will think they're still dreaming when they wake up and see *you!*"